Richard

ROBIN OF SHERWOOD

QUEEN OF THE
BLACK SUN

Richard Carpenter's Robin of Sherwood
Queen of the Black Sun
Written by Kenton Hall
From an idea by Iain Meadows

First published in 2021
(as part of the Series 4 Collection)

This new edition
Published in 2024 by
Chinbeard Books

in association with
Oak Tree Books
oaktreebooks.uk

Editor: Barnaby Eaton-Jones
Range Consultant: Harriet Whitehouse

Robin of Sherwood TV Series
created by Richard Carpenter
Copyright © 1983 HTV/Goldcrest Films & TV

Richard Carpenter's

ROBIN OF SHERWOOD

QUEEN OF THE BLACK SUN

by

Kenton Hall

A Chinbeard Books / Oak Tree Books Original

PROLOGUE

The storm had been fierce, almost vengeful, and, though lasting only a single night, had felt like the end of days.

Rain, whipped into a frenzy by a cold, hard wind, had beaten the ground like a tantrumming child while, in the forest, trees that had held ground for centuries found themselves shorn, even uprooted by the maelstrom.

The outlaws were more prepared than most perhaps, but those who inhabited the greenwood had not escaped entirely unscathed—there would be much work to do over the coming weeks.

Marion's heart went out to the villages surrounding their outlaw home. To those villagers who already paid so dearly for their hardscrabble existence yet found space for love and light and joy regardless. To fear the violent attentions of the sheriff's men was bad enough, but to have Nature herself turn upon you seemed a cruel joke.

This too, the guardians of Sherwood would set themselves to right.

It was a bracing thought, as it often was when the young woman's mind turned to the injustices around every corner—nimbly dodging her own heartache—and it straightened her back as she picked her way gingerly over broken branches and trudged through patches of thick, sucking mud.

The sky above was cloudless and blue, as if apologising for its previous misdemeanours. The air felt electric and smelt sweet.

There was magic in it.

Not a thought that Marion ever imagined she would take literally, but she had seen so many things since her old life ended and this new one began. Though in truth, that first new life had also fallen, leaving in its place something more painful but, perhaps, with the added purity of having tasted the flame.

This forest, this *land*, was once a refuge—a place to which she'd fled: for freedom, for honour, for love. Now she was one with it. It had become her second bridegroom.

And so, today, she would do her utmost to ease its pain.

'Over here,' shouted Will Scarlet, from just over a low rise ahead. He shook his head in angry frustration. 'Will you look at the state of that…'

'Now,' a voice seemed to say. Whether it had been in her mind or carried on the remaining wind, she couldn't say for certain, but it tugged at her regardless.

Marion shook off her reveries of the past and quickened her pace.

On the other side of the rise, the cause of Will's consternation quickly became apparent.

The valley, yesterday as familiar to Marion as any previous home could have been, looked as though it had slipped into some grotesquery: a costume to frighten children. Familiar shapes lurked beneath distressed and unsettling garb, all the more frightening for the few elements that remained untouched.

Look.

A landslip had cut away at the hillside opposite; the heavy rain had sloughed the earth itself away, revealing a slender opening into its very bowels. She could see Will, John, Much and Robin ahead of her, stood around the rift, staring into its heart.

It felt, Marion thought, alive. Alive but wounded. Like the forest itself.

She stopped in her tracks a short distance away to get the lay of the land.

'A cave?' she heard Little John say.

'Well done, John,' replied Will.

'I was just saying, lad.'

'Well, it's hardly likely to be an apothecary's, is it?'

'Why would there be an apothecary in the side of a hill?' asked Much. 'They wouldn't get much business if they were hidden away like that.'

Will opened his mouth to respond to Much's comment, but Robin placed a calming hand on his shoulder.

'No, they wouldn't, Much.'

Marion smiled. The lad had grown so much since the man he called brother had died, and he had taken to the fair-haired successor with an open heart. Even battling through his grief, whilst learning to trust their new leader, Much had retained an innocence that had held this band together as often as any adventure—or misadventure—shared.

Daughter of the Forest! Come!

Marion felt the commanded invitation run through her.

4

Little John took a step closer to the damaged ground. 'Look at the size of it. No man's getting in there.'

I call you. Will you answer?

'No man, perhaps, John.'

The four men turned towards Marion; three faces clouded with confusion and the fourth with concern.

'No,' said Robin, simply.

'Robin—' she began, though unsure what more she could say. She knew that Robin was concerned for her safety, that he knew better than most what she had lost and, in many ways, what he had gained. Nonetheless, it was not mere safety she desired, but security—and that was something she must fight for, beneath her own banner—in addition to his, to theirs.

Robin Hood paused, watching her eyes. 'Marion,' he said, a note of suspicion colouring his voice. 'What is it?'

'Do you trust me?'

'You know I do.'

'And have I ever doubted Herne's son?'

Robin laughed and almost immediately regretted it.

'When it truly mattered,' added Marion with a small but determined smile.

The remaining outlaws had taken a few steps back towards the cave's mouth, wise enough not to get involved. Robin looked over his shoulder, giving their cowardice a hard stare. Will shrugged back at him. Little John stifled a grin.

Much, by contrast, looked upset. He had never cared for conflict. He'd seen too much of it in his young life. He'd rally in a fight, but he never quite knew what to do during a personal dispute. Especially between Robin and Marion.

'No, you've never doubted Herne's Son.' admitted Robin.

'Then you must show me the same courtesy. You either trust me—without question, as you trust the others—or you don't.'

He knew she was right and said so, with little further hesitation. Then a thought struck him and his face brightened.

'Would I send any of the others alone into the dark?'

Marion's face fell. Whoever was reaching out for her had called her alone.

'No,' she conceded.

'Then Much will accompany you.'

'Me?' blurted Much. 'In there?'

Robin turned.

'I'd send John, but half of him alone would seal the entrance.'

'It's what you get for being small,' Will gave the young man a nudge.

'I'm not small,' said Much, straightening proudly.

'Are you not?' said Little John, stepping closer to him.

Much glared up at him.

'We can't all be giants.'

'What you lack in stature,' said Robin, himself trying not to laugh, 'you more than make up for in spirit. And you wouldn't let Marion investigate in there alone, would you?'

'Of course not!'

'Then it's decided. Marion and Much will enter and we will keep watch.'

'But we won't be able to see anything.'

'You'll take torches,' said Robin who, now that the decision had been reached, had once more taken the reins. If he couldn't lead the party then he would lead the defence. 'And we'll keep our own lit from the cave's mouth.'

Marion reached out to the voice. Is this your will?

Approach. You and the one who would your protector be.

This last sentence rankled somewhat. We protect each other, she thought. But she knew she'd go.

'Right,' she said aloud. 'Come on then, Much. There's a mystery to unravel.'

Much trudged, unenthusiastically, to her side, peering into the shadows of the cave.

'I don't like mysteries,' he said. 'There always seems to be a sword at the end of them.'

'Unless they're arming rats, lad…' John started.

'*Rats?*'

'Leave him be,' said Robin. And then to Marion: 'Be safe.'

She saw the flicker of fear in his eyes and wished that she could explain. Explain that she felt safer in this moment than she had in some time.

But he would have to see it for himself to believe it.

CHAPTER 1

The entrance remained uncomfortably narrow for several feet, though it felt much longer to Much as they edged their way further into the cave. Marion led the way, her footing far surer than that of the miller's son.

Had Much been concentrating on anything other than keeping his fear at bay and his eye out for Little John's threatened rats, her haste might have seemed reckless at best, irresponsible at worst and worrisome in either case. Yet, even if he had been aware, he would not have seen the invisible hand that Marion felt at her back, ushering ever forwards.

Though she was aware that she was being led, Marion felt little fear. Or rather, she felt fear mingled with joy, as though travelling to meet a lover for the first time. She wondered idly if this was what it had been like for Robin—Robin of Loxley—the first time he came before Herne. Was she about to receive her own calling, her own destiny? And would it preclude the one she had chosen for herself?

'Marion,' whispered Much.

'I don't think you need to whisper, Much.' She replied without turning, though she found her own voice not much louder.

'What if this doesn't lead anywhere? What if it's just a crack in the world?'

'Then we'll turn back,' she reassured him. 'There are torches at our back and friends waiting. We'll come to no harm. Besides, look—'

Ahead of them they could see a twist in the shape of the shadows cast by their torches. A gradual widening of the passage into a large, cavernous chamber that—though it could not have been, surely—appeared to have been cut by human hands. By masters of the craft, at any rate. Gone were the gnarled tendrils of tree roots, the spattering of grit and gravel amongst the mud and underlying bedrock. The stone here was far more perfectly hewn than nature preferred.

Marion pulled herself along the passage-way as fast as the space would allow and all but burst into the cavern, holding her torch high in anticipation.

Much followed more reluctantly, a hesitation that seemed borne out as the features of the chamber came into focus in the light.

A circle of stone caskets surrounded what could only be an altar—strewn with bones wrapped haphazardly in age-worn rags. The entire space radiated ritual and sacrifice.

'A burial chamber,' breathed Marion.

Much abruptly stopped worrying about rats and pulled at Marion's arm.

'We shouldn't be 'ere,' he said. 'Nothing good comes of a place like this.'

Marion turned, her face lit eerily by the torch.

'Oh Much!' She shook her head. 'Don't be silly. Whoever used this place is long gone, sealed away for who knows how long. There's nothing to be afraid of.'

'That's what someone always says, right before something bad 'appens.'

'Who's to say this wasn't a holy site? A place of protection?'

Much looked around with distaste.

'I doubt Tuck would consider it very holy.'

Marion laughed. 'I'm not sure Tuck is the best judge of that.'

'You have come.' The voice said, both within Marion's mind and without, echoing around the chamber. Though, from her companion's lack of reaction, apparently for her ears only.

'I have come,' she confirmed, beneath her breath.

'What was that?' Much, who was circling the ring of caskets uneasily, swung round to face Marion.

'Nothing.' She felt a pang of guilt at her deception, but this was not a secret she felt entitled to share. 'Come on, let's see what's here.' She hurried over to the nearest casket and gave the heavy stone lid an experimental shove. 'Can you help me please, Much?'

But even as the words left her lips, she felt the stone give way, its seal breaking with a thunderous rumble. Both Marion and Much felt a shiver dash the lengths of their spines; Marion's confidence dimmed.

'I think we should go,' said Much. 'I don't think we're... alone here.'

But Marion shook her head. They'd come this far. She was so sure this was the right thing to do— although she didn't know why.

Stepping forward, she peered over the lip of the casket. Within lay a bounty unlike any she had ever seen. No errant knight or tax collector caught in the forest could ever have concealed this about their person. Gold and silver coins, by their hundreds. Jewels of every cut and hue. And nestled amongst them, an obsidian gemstone of such rich blackness that it seemed to steal light from their torches.

'Oh!' Much's mouth dropped open in awed surprise.

The light bounced between the torch and the shadowy gemstone, glimmering briefly in Marion's eyes as though taking root, before extinguishing just as rapidly.

She reached out for the stone, fascinated by its size and the sheer solidity of it. It felt lighter than she'd imagined as she grasped it. But it quickly grew lighter still—crumbling to dust in her palm, despite the reverence of her hold on it.

Marion gasped in surprise.

'Fake,' said Much. 'I should have known.' He grasped at a handful of coins in disgust, but they proved to be far more substantial. He shuffled a gold one between two fingers and raised it to his mouth. A brief, exploratory bite lightened his mood.

'They're real.'

He looked again at the number of coins still filling the open casket.

'If they're *all* real—'

'I know, Much. I know.'

'All the people we could help—' The young man trailed off, the thought of the good that could be done overwhelming him. Then his eyes found the altar again, the bones. 'Maybe it's a trick,' he added warily.

'A trick?'

'Like in stories. The gods want to see if you're greedy or mean, so they leave cursed gifts. We could take all that back to Sherwood and it could be the end of us.'

Marion genuinely considered this. Tests of courage, of worthiness were certainly not unheard of, and the old gods were not something she thought of in the abstract. Not anymore.

'Then perhaps we should turn it over to the sheriff. I can't think of anyone more deserving of a curse.'

Much wrinkled his nose.

'He'd probably like being cursed. He'd rob the Devil, then sell his own horns back to him.' His mouth puckered as he tried to justify this to himself. 'Maybe if it went to the poor, the curse would be broken.'

'Maybe. And if it is a test, then it simply must be passed. We have to prove ourselves worthy. That's usually how the story goes, isn't it?'

As Marion spoke, the light that had glinted in her eyes came roaring back to life. She felt it blossom and turned her head to keep it from Much's concerned gaze.

Something was waking. Or had already woken. Silently, she cried out to the voice that had summoned her here: *You asked me to come. You called me daughter.*

She heard the voice in response: *I called you Daughter of the Forest. I am not the forest.*

Marion felt a pressure in her chest as her strength momentarily left her. Her knees buckled and she grasped at the casket to steady herself.

'Marion!' Much ran to her side. 'What's wrong?'

When she straightened, all sign of weakness had gone. She smiled gently, cupping his cheek with her hand.

'I'm alright, Much. The air in here is thin, that's all. Let's see what we can do about getting this back to the others. Then we can make a decision together.'

This appeased Much, although he couldn't shake his suspicions. But he knew Robin would know what to do.

He always knew.

Outside the entrance, Robin paced, deep in thought, as the others took turns lighting a path back to Sherwood for their absent friends.

Little John watched his leader for a while before reaching a decision. He marched over and clapped an enormous palm on each of Robin's shoulders, stopping his pacing in its tracks.

'She'll be fine, Robin.'

'I know that. Much is with her, and—'

John laughed. 'Much is a grown man now Robin, that's true enough, But I'm sure he feels safer because he's with Marion, rather than the other way around. She's as strong and as fierce—fiercer, than any of us. Every time we've lost her, by fair means or foul, she's found her way back. And she will this time too. Besides—' He released Robin and rubbed his hands together. '—who knows what treasures she'll stumble upon? We might have to consider having a Queen in Sherwood, rather a King.'

Robin shook his head, but his friend's counsel had reached its target.

'Do you imagine she'd be as merciful as I about your tendency to go your own way when you think you know best?' He leaned in and gave a sniff of the heavy fur at Little John's shoulder with a sudden smile. 'Or your smell?'

'Give over.' He gave Robin a playful shove.

Robin was about to shove John back, when they heard a low rumble. It seemed to be coming from inside the cave. Robin and Little John exchanged a look of panic and ran towards the others.

The sound came again, this time surrounding them. As though an army of horseman were galloping at them from all sides.

'I think it's thunder,' said Will, looking up to see dark, sodden clouds rolling in above them, at an unnatural pace.

'Now who's stating the obvious?' Little John let his rejoinder fly almost without thought, his eyes darting across the suddenly pitch-black sky.

'This is not the work of nature,' said Robin as the ground shook beneath their feet. He offered a silent prayer to Herne for the protection of everyone in Sherwood.

And then the rains returned. Heavier than even the night before, slashing down at them like knives.

'Cover! Get to cover!' Robin bellowed.

'But Marion!' Will yelled from the cave mouth, his torch already extinguished by the downpour.

'Much! They're down there!'

'We're no good to them if we don't find shelter.' Robin replied, though the words caught in his throat as he tried to banish thoughts of the water filling the gap in the earth, and working its way to their friends. Trapping them. Or worse.

Will growled, frustrated that he couldn't do anything to help Marion or Much as he joined the others, following as they moved swiftly over the hillside towards a welcoming patch of dense trees.

John stumbled as they crested the hill, his ankle turning into the newly slick mud, and tumbled— debris following him in wide, angry rivulets—back to where they had begun. He cursed as he slid to a halt and struggled back to his feet.

'Come on, John!' shouted Will.

'Wait! Robin, wait!'

Robin knew the frightened tone in John's voice well enough to stop moving. 'What is it?'

But as he turned his gaze back towards the incline and looked down towards the cave's mouth, he saw exactly what it was. The storm was determined to finish its work. Or rather, undo it.

Clumps of soil were detaching further from the hillside, stones tumbling in their wake. All following

18

a path towards the narrow crevice Marion and Much had entered.

Whatever door it was that the previous storm had opened, it was being forced closed again. With their friends inside.

Half-running, half-falling, Robin made his way back down the hillside; scrambling to the cave. He kicked at stones and vainly attempted to claw the thickening mud from the opening with both hands. John and Will, hot on his heels, wedged themselves either side of the crack, hoping against reason to somehow stem the tide.

'Marion! Much!' Robin's voice felt ragged in his throat as he screamed into the darkness. 'MARION!'

Marion walked the length of a second stone casket, back and forth, occasionally dipping to one knee to examine it from another angle. Then she walked to one end and wedged her torch upright into the pile of coins.

Taking a deep breath, she bent, grasped the corners firmly and lifted. It was heavier than the last one, but not immovable. It rose briefly before her hands gave way and it fell back in place with a thump. Marion sighed and dusted her hands together.

'Much, give me a hand with this. Maybe between the two of us—'

But Much was distracted, staring intently back the way they'd come.

'Did you hear something?'

Marion paused, listening.

'I don't think so.'

'I'm sure I heard Robin shouting.'

'I think you're imagining things. Can you help me get this to the cave mouth? If we can shift it towards the entrance, we can call to the others to fetch us something to carry the coins in.'

'Okay.' Much turned back to Marion, 'you'll need a purse larger than I've ever seen for this lot.'

'We'll find a way. Now help me lift.'

Much repeated Marion's trick with the torch and took hold of the opposite end of the casket.

'One, two—' Marion squared her shoulders. 'Three.'

They strained every sinew, but even together they could do little more but raise the stone slightly and briefly.

'It's no good,' said Much.

'We can't leave all of this behind. Knowing what could be accomplished with it.' Marion reclaimed her torch and circled the room. 'Perhaps there's something here that we could carry the treasure in.'

She felt her way around the walls, hand trailing lightly against the stone, until she gave a cry of triumph.

'What is it?'

'Another passage.'

Marion bit her lip.

'It's not as wide as the other one, but I think I can make it.'

'If you get trapped… Robin will have my hide.'

'I best not get trapped then.'

'Marion, please. Let's just go. Maybe we should talk to the others first?'

She marched over to the young man and took his chin in her hand.

'Much, how many times have you complained to me that you're always being given orders? That you never get to decide on a plan of action yourself?'

'Yes, but this is just you giving me orders. I think—'

'I won't be long. Wait here and if I don't come back, you have my full permission to run for help.'

Much hesitated. He didn't like it, but he also knew he was unlikely to convince Marion otherwise if she had set her mind to something. He nodded unhappily.

'I'll return, before you even realise I've gone.'

Clasping her torch in one hand, she squeezed into the narrow opening and began to shuffle along it.

I bet she's heading towards danger, thought Much. *It's always danger.*

Then he heard it gain. Much strained his ears. Robin's voice was calling to them. They weren't that far from the cave's mouth, yet it sounded distant and strained.

'Marion! Much!' The words finally struggled into the cavern. 'You have to get out of there! Now!'

Much blanched, almost frozen in place by exactly what he feared most. He darted to the second opening and peered in. Nothing but shadow. Not even the flicker of Marion's torch.

'Marion! Robin says we have to leave! Something's wrong!'

Nothing. The silence was thick, as though it was swallowing any words that came too close.

Robin's voice came again. 'Much! Can you hear me? Get out! Both of you!'

The young man found himself torn between the eerie hush and his panic-stricken leader. He'd have to go in after Marion. He'd have to. He couldn't leave without her. He couldn't abandon her here. Never mind what Robin would do to him, he'd never be able to live with it.

'We're coming!' Much shouted back towards the mouth of the cave, hoping the others could hear him.

He took a breath and began to ease his shoulder into the crevice. He'd find her, get them both out. *It will be fine. It will all be fine.*

But then there was the scream. For a moment, Much thought the sound might have been coming from his own throat, until he recognised Marion's voice.

'Much!' The cry of pain and panic ripped through the miller's son.

'Marion? Are you alright? I'm coming to get you!'

'No!' the wail continued. 'You have to run! There are devils here! Devils in the dark!'

'Devils? What devils?'

'Find Robin! Quickly!'

'But I can't leave you here—'

'Run, Much, run!'

23

As if the distant Marion had exhaled one final breath, a gust of wind drove out of the depths of the opening and extinguished Much's torch.

And he ran.

CHAPTER 2

'There he is!'

Will fought his way forward to grab Much's shoulder and pull him free of the rapidly closing cave. They stumbled backwards on the slick ground and fell with a thud, as John and Robin took their place, clearly expecting Marion to appear behind Much.

The rain was falling in thick sheets now, and it was getting difficult to see more than a few inches in front of their faces.

Robin spun towards Much as he struggled to his feet.

'Where is Marion?' he yelled over the storm. 'What happened in there?'

'There were devils, Robin. Coming for us.' Much was babbling, his tears even heavier than the rain. 'She told me I had to run. She made me.'

'You left her?' Robin was incandescent with anger.

'I didn't want to. But she said, and… Devils. Devils in the dark.'

'What are you talking about? What devils?'

But Much was out of words, his whole body was shaking.

'Robin!' John shouted from the opening to the cave. 'We're running out of time.'

Lifting their eyes to the landscape, the outlaws could see the hillside was continuing to break up. The cave's mouth was in genuine danger of being returned to its tomb—with Marion still inside.

'You have to go back!' Robin grabbed Much roughly by the arm and dragged him towards the cave. 'You're the only one who can.'

'I can't!' pleaded Much. 'Don't make me, Robin. Please. Don't make me.'

'You'd rather leave Marion to die?'

The war between fear and fealty waged across the young man's features and, even in his anguish, Robin felt a pang of guilt. But he couldn't afford it. Not with Marion in danger.

He took Much's shoulder and marched him to where Little John and Will were trying in vain to hold back the tide of earth and stone that threatened to smother Marion's only way out.

'Do you see that? If you don't go back, she will be sealed away. Alive or dead, we will never see her again.'

'Marion!'

'Yes, Much. Marion.'

'No,' said Much, extending a trembling finger. 'Marion!'

And then Robin saw it too, the figure, head down—a bundle clasped tightly in its arms—struggling free of the cave's mouth.

'John! Will!'

The two men, careless of the sharp stone edges that tore at their hands, pulled Marion free. The force of their panic sending all three of them tumbling down the hill just as the elements took over and the cave was removed from the world as swiftly as it had revealed.

There was little time to celebrate the reunion; they hastened through the forest in an attempt to reach camp before the storm became any more severe. They travelled in silence through the thick air as the unending rain continued its quest to confuse their senses and dull their spirits.

Robin, a few steps ahead, scouted for a landmark by which to navigate. He and Marion had not spoken since her miraculous escape and the others daren't bring the subject up, for fear of an eruption that would make no concessions to innocent bystanders.

Much, however, had not been able to drag his eyes from Marion's face, nor from the bundle in her arms. He knew what it must be, but she had barely acknowledged him since she returned.

Finally, he could stand it no longer. 'How did you escape?' he whispered.

Marion turned, a cold look on her face.

'What do you mean? The same way you did, I imagine. Although I'd like to think I might have waited for you, had the positions been reversed.'

Much recoiled, his words hitting him as if she'd slapped him around the face.

'You told me I had to run.'

'I said no such thing. I found my way back, just as I said I would, and you were gone.'

'No, that's not right.' Much was grief-stricken that she could even believe such a thing. He couldn't. He wouldn't.

'But the devils—' he began.

Marion stopped walking.

'Devils?'

'You shouted to me. Told me there were devils in the dark.'

In his sorrow, Much didn't notice Marion's brief

hesitation before she replied. 'I think your mind was playing tricks on you.' Her voice softened slightly. 'I'd have been frightened too.'

'I would never have left you if—'

'I know. Put it out of your mind, Much. We're here now. And—'

She pulled at the corner of the rags in her arms, revealing the glint of precious metal concealed beneath.

'—we have something to show for our adventures.'

Robin stopped walking, waiting for the group to catch him up. His face was pained.

'It's no good. I can't see further than my own hand in this rain. I think we need to find shelter and wait the storm out.'

'How are we lost?' Will raked a hand through his sodden hair. 'We were barely two hours from camp.'

'How does anyone get lost?' Little John grunted.

'What's that supposed to mean?'

'Well, we obviously took the wrong path. Maybe if you'd been paying more attention—'

'Me?' Will glowered, 'How come it's always down to me when—'

'Enough!' Robin shouted, not needing his friends' frustration at their situation to boil over

29

until they'd at least found some shelter. 'I saw some caves just ahead. They'll be dry and they'll be out of the wind.'

'Haven't we had enough of caves?'

'If you have a better idea, Will, I'm happy to hear it.'

Will Scarlet grimaced. 'If we get buried alive, it'll be on your head. That's all I'm saying.'

Later that night, as they sat huddled around a small fire—steam rising in clouds from their rain-sodden garments—Marion laid out what she and Much had discovered in the cavern.

Will, who had spent much of the previous few hours eyeing the entrance to the cave as if expecting to catch it up to something, leapt forward at the sight of the coins.

'There were more,' said Marion. 'But I had to find something to carry them out in, and this was as much as I could manage.'

'Is it real?' asked Will.

Much nodded. 'There was silver as well. And jewels.'

For a moment, Will's face fell at the thought of what had been left behind, but the sight of the firelight shimmering from the pile of coins soon remedied that.

Robin reached forward and took a coin in hand. 'No markings,' he mused.

He held the coin up for the others to see. It was true. No inscriptions, simply perfectly smooth discs of gold.

'Might have been stolen,' suggested Little John. 'Melted down and recast. Gold is gold, after all.'

'Stolen. Quite possibly. But who from?' Robin stood to stretch his legs.

'God knows how long it's been shut up in that cave,' said Will. 'I don't think whoever it was is coming back for it.'

'You said it looked like a burial chamber, Marion?'

'Yes.' Marion's head snapped up, as if surprised to be addressed. She'd looked paler since her return. Quieter, certainly. As though she weren't entirely with them. She claimed that she felt quite well and was simply tired, but Robin wasn't so sure.

'So the real question is whose grave did we just rob?' Much eyed the money suspiciously. 'And will they mind?'

Will was on his feet now too. Pacing the cave as he muttered, 'For God's sake. We rob the living often enough. I think the dead'll probably mind less.'

'After all we've seen, Will? Is that risk you're prepared to take?' Robin frowned thoughtfully.

'For that much gold? Yes. Twice over.'

Robin held his tongue. Their shelter was too small for any further dispute. He tucked a coin into his jerkin.

'I must speak to Herne. Then we'll decide what to do with it.'

Will held up his hands in surrender.

'Fine. Even the spirit of the forest is going to be hard-pressed to turn down a gift like this.'

Conversation slowly dried, as they stretched themselves across the stone floor, in search of an uncomfortable but essential night's sleep.

Marion's weariness was bone-deep but she could feel herself resisting slumber. As she lay, her head resting on her hands, she realised she could hear a voice singing softly in the distance. The same voice she had heard before.

It had a woman's cadence, but its gentleness masked a darker intent. Yet—at the same time—it was soothing. Inviting.

Marion sat up, listening more intently. She longed to run towards it.

'*Feed*,' the voice said. '*Feed the Black Sun.*'

The next morning they were woken by a familiar voice.

'Robin?' it called out. 'Little Flower?'

Then a face to match, peering into the blackness of the cave.

'Oh, thank heavens,' said Friar Tuck. 'We feared the worst.' He crossed himself in gratitude. Behind him, came Nasir, calm and silent as always, a hint of a smile the only sign that he too had shed a weight of apprehension.

Robin, John, Will and Much shook off the last remnants of sleep, stretching and scratching themselves back to life.

'Marion, wake up. Tuck and Nasir have come for us.' Much nudged Marion's foot with his own, his mood lightened greatly by the arrival of his friends.

There was no response.

'Marion?'

He tilted his face towards her lips. There was breath, but no other sign of life.

'Robin, she won't wake up.'

Suddenly apprehensive, Robin knelt at her side and shook her as gently as he could.

'Marion.' He shook her again, more urgently. 'Marion!' He turned pleadingly to the newcomers. 'Tuck. Something's wrong.'

'Give me some room,' said the friar, ushering the others out of the cave and joining Robin at Marion's side. He too failed to rouse her, no matter the number of silent prayers he uttered.

'What happened to her?'

'She was very nearly buried alive,' Robin admitted.

'I'd call that a very good reason to sleep deeply,' said Tuck, sounding unconvinced. 'I'm sure she just needs her rest.'

'Nothing is sure about this,' said the Hooded Man. 'Nothing at all. I must speak to Herne. We don't know what we're up against here.'

'Again?' shouted Scarlet from the entrance.

'Quiet, Will!' barked Robin. 'I'm trying to think.'

'While you're thinking,' came Little John's voice, 'you'd best come and have a look at this.'

Robin and Tuck joined the others at the mouth of the cave. The friar immediately crossed himself.

'Was it like this when you came to find us?' asked Robin.

Nasir shook his head, his eyes narrowed and body tense. 'It's not been like *this* before.'

34

Where there had been blue skies and calm—then rain and devastation—there was now a thick blanket of fog. In fact, fog seemed too earthbound and ordinary a word of it. It was as though the storm and the night had become one—the world lost from sight, each breath haunted by the ghost of drowning.

Nasir withdrew a blade and passed it slowly back and forth, cutting the air. There was resistance, as though his swords moving through flesh.

'This is not of nature.'

Will pointed upwards. 'I'd be more concerned about that.'

There in the sky, improbably visible through the fog, hung the sun. Eclipsed—a thin, blazing corona of light at its edges.

'An ill omen,' whispered Tuck. 'An ill omen, indeed.'

'And there was me imagining it a blessing.'

'Will—' cautioned Robin.

'We need to get back to camp.'

'Agreed, Much. But we lost our way in the storm alone. Where would we end up in this?'

'Hell,' said Little John darkly.

Friar Tuck began to intone a prayer under his breath. He moved back to Marion's side and laid a comforting hand on her brow.

Robin became aware of a warmth spreading from the hilt at his waist.

Albion was glowing—pulsing with heat.

'We are still Herne's people and I am still Herne's son. If this is an attack from a source beyond our understanding, then it is he who shall deliver us from it. I must go to him. Alone.'

'You're not planning to go out in that?' said Little John in disbelief. 'We just agreed we'd get lost again.'

'What choice do I have?'

'To *not* go out in that?'

'And we what? Wait here to die while Marion labours beneath some spell?'

'Then take us with you.'

'John, I trust you to watch over Marion. Over Much and the others. It is my responsibility to find Herne and hear his words.'

'But Robin—'

'I have your trust?'

Little John ground his teeth but nodded.

'Then I shall be in good company.'

Robin turned to face the others. 'We will be together in Sherwood again. Watch out for each other.' He nodded towards the still-sleeping Marion. 'I know I don't have to ask you to look after her.'

Then he drew Albion and stepped into the fog, disappearing from sight almost as soon as his foot crossed the cave's threshold.

John growled in frustration. The inaction was burning in his stomach.

'Robin!' he called out. 'Wait!'

If Robin Hood heard them, he gave no reply.

'Do you hear that?' said Will.

'What?' replied John, craning forward.

'Nothing.'

'He's right,' said Tuck. 'No birds. No life.'

When you lived as part of the forest, its daily sounds fell into the background, like the air, precious but unmarked. But now, true silence reigned, bar a thin, whistling wind that gave no comfort at all.

'To hell with this,' said Little John. 'I'm not leaving him alone out there in that. Herne's son or not. Tuck, look after Marion. Much, look after Tuck. Nasir, Will, I'm going after Robin. Am I going alone?'

Nasir sheathed his sword and widened his stance. Will gripped the hilt of his own until his knuckles showed white.

John nodded.

'That's what I thought. Come on, lads. No fog is taking down Robin Hood's men.'

Robin took one careful step after the other, trusting that the still glowing blade of Albion at his side would guide his feet. His eyes certainly could not be trusted. He may as well have been standing still for all the difference each step made. Even the ground beneath him felt wrong, insubstantial.

Herne, he thought. Do not forsake your son.

The answer came swiftly.

Have you forgotten the forest you protect?

The forest has forgotten me, Robin thought as he replied, 'I seek it. But it evades me.'

Or you evade it, too distracted to hear its call. Focus, Robin i'the Hood. Call Sherwood to you. It will come. Forget what you see and cannot see. Concentrate on what you know.

Robin closed his eyes and drew Albion, holding it before him like a divining rod.

He could feel the heat from its blade increase, his face glowing in the borrowed rays of the absent sun.

Then he stepped forward.

He felt it, even before he opened his eyes. The fog had lifted. Or he had been led from it. Either way, the green of Sherwood Forest—untouched by fog or storm—made his heart leap briefly in his chest. The ache remained, but hope was a much-needed balm.

As was the sight of Herne the Hunter.

It felt, at times, as though he had never seen Herne whole but, rather, in a series of impressions. A silhouette. A pair of arms outstretched in blessing or warning. Proud antlers framing a hidden face.

Yet here was Herne complete. Robin knew, in his mind, there was a man beneath the god's burden. But, in his heart, his faith was seldom tested.

'We have not much time,' Herne said. 'An ancient evil has risen. One I cannot fell. A power older even than the trees, broken free of its confinement.'

Robin felt a sudden burning sensation on his skin. He reached into his jerkin and his hand found the mysterious, faceless coin. It was oddly cold to the touch but hissed like fire against his skin.

'This was found,' he said. 'And I fear we may lose the finder.'

Herne contemplated the coin in eerie silence.

Finally, he spoke:

'There will be a loss, Herne's son. You have a weakness and it must be faced.'

'What weakness?'

'The fear my words have dragged, even now, into your breast.'

CHAPTER 3

'Oh, Little Flower,' murmured Tuck, his hand on Marion's brow.

Her face, still pale, was beaded with sweat. The fever had come on soon after the others had departed. As soon as Robin had departed, Tuck added to himself.

'We need to find some water,' he called to Much, who was anxiously manning the mouth of the cave. 'Or we may lose her.'

Much stared into the fog through which his friends had disappeared. He felt a coward for even hesitating, but Tuck was already at his side, his face a picture of understanding.

'You, my young friend, have faced enough devils for the day. I'll go. There was a river nearby. Unless the forest itself has moved, I think I can find it.

Once I have found it, I'll call for you and you can guide me back.'

Grateful for such kindness, Much straightened.

Tuck withdrew a leather skin water pouch from beneath the large rope belt that encircled his waist. "Keep her safe, as best you can.'

Robin was ashamed to admit it, but he found his patience growing thin. He wanted to fight something, to teach something a thorough lesson for the suffering it had put his people through, put Marion through.

But he knew too well that Herne's words might be the shield that kept an arrow from his heart and so swallowed his fury, and so he listened.

'What is man's greatest weakness?' Herne asked.

This took no consideration at all. Robin's life had been at its mercy from a child.

'Greed. The desire to have what he has not got.'

Herne nodded. He seemed pleased, like a father whose child has repeated a word cleanly and clearly.

'This is the danger you face. That you have always faced and will face again. There was a time, outside of living memory, yet not completely forgotten, when man found balance and climbed out of the darkness. For a great power fed on their greed and in warring against it, they saw the path clearly. They extinguished prey and hunter as one.'

Robin let the images wash over him. As ever, when he communed with Herne, he felt he understood nothing and everything all at once.

'A prison was built to contain this power, a reminder to never again raise the crop upon which it fed. A circle of gold and silver, imbued with the power to vanquish the darkness and embolden the light. But the ages passed and humankind once more found themselves corrupted by the disease of greed. The servants of light and darkness alike. Now only Herne and Herne's son stand as gatekeepers of the path. The path created of each man's weakness. A fear that they must face and conquer.'

'What must I do?' It was as much a plea for clarity as it was for guidance, but Herne's tale had concluded. He was already retreating, back into the forest.

'Much!'

Marion's voice, from the back of the cave, startled him. He'd begun to grow sickeningly accustomed to the intense silence and, for a moment, his mind refused to align the sound with the idea that she had finally woken.

'Much! Help me! Where am I?'

As he rushed to her side, wiping her fevered cheeks, it briefly occurred to him to ask himself why, out of his sight, his name was upon her lips. She would call for Robin first, surely? Perhaps she had never truly left that cavern awake? Whatever spirit had overtaken her, perhaps she was finally released?

He looked towards the entrance to the cave, but only darkness met him. Enveloping him as surely as the fog had done the others.

And in the darkness, Marion's voice came again. 'Devils, Much. Devils in the dark.'

'No!'

'They took me, Much. Dragged me into the shadows.'

'Marion, please. Stop.'

'*Feed.*'

'What?'

'*Feed the black sun.*'

Much found himself moving towards the voice.

Even as his mind screamed at him to flee, he reached forward—closer to the words.

Feed, he thought. *Feed the black sun.*

'Nasir!' called Will Scarlet. 'You're the tracker. Can't you find anything to go on?'

They'd been making their way through the fog for what felt like hours. For all Will knew, they'd been travelling in smaller and smaller circles, and they'd be tripping over each other before long.

In his irritation, it took him a moment to notice that Nasir had not replied.

Scarlet whirled in the fog, hoping not to discover what he feared he would.

He was alone.

'Nasir! John!' he shouted.

As he grimly expected, he heard nothing. Even his own voice sound thin and unreal.

He closed his eyes and breathed deeply. This was nothing. It was fog. He'd killed more men than he could count, all of whom had been equally intent on dispatching him. No mist was going to take him down.

Wait. There was something.

'Will! Thank heaven!'

Marion's voice? She was awake. Probably blundered past Much, hoping to chase after Robin.

'Marion. Stay where you are. I'll follow your voice.'

'Yes, Will. Follow my voice.'

He moved towards the sound, hand outstretched. 'I can't find you. Keep talking.'

'I'm here.'

No, that wasn't right. The voice was behind him now. He turned.

'Don't be afraid,' he said, though to whom he was no longer sure. 'I'm close. I have to be.'

'Where's Robin?'

Will sighed. Of course she'd be asking about Robin. Not him; the idiot scrabbling around in the fog trying to find her.

'He's gone to see Herne. You were sleeping. We didn't know what else to do.'

'The gatekeeper has the key.'

This last sentence didn't appear to be directed at him and, feeling his nerves jangle, he drew his sword.

'Marion. Everything's fine. We just need to find each other, get back to the cave and wait out this fog. Robin will find Herne and it'll all be sorted.'

'There's something in the mist, Will.'

Will gripped his sword tighter.

'Whatever it is, I'll take care of it.'

'How, Will? How are you going to take care of it?'

'Don't I always?'

'Did you take care of *her*?'

The fog seemed to contract, the temperature dropping into Will felt as though he were about to be encased in ice.

'What did you say?'

No reply.

'Who are you?'

'You know who I am. I'm afraid, Will.'

No more. No more of this. Scarlet lifted his sword and took the hilt in both hands. And then watched in horrified fascination as the blade crumbled from the tip down, dissipating into the fog, leaving nothing in his fingers but a twisted, shapeless lump of metal.

'No!' he screamed. 'No! Not that!'

Will crashed to his knees against the forest floor, staring at the space where his sword had been.

'You can't take that. Not that! How can I fight now? What good will I be to anyone without it?' The words were peeled from him like skin from the back of a flayed man.

'Be calm, Will,' said Marion's voice.

But he was babbling now.

'I'll need a blacksmith. Yes, I'll find a village, find a blacksmith, they'll repair it. Then I can protect you. Protect you all.'

'*Bathe your wounds in light of the black sun*,' came the reply. '*Feed the black sun.*'

Nasir kept himself low to the ground, trying to ignore any senses that seemed intent on misleading him—relying on instinct alone.

It was his instinct, after all, that had led him to this life.

Nonetheless, it was an uncomfortable experience, feeling cut off from the almost endless minute signs of life on which he predicated his gift. He knew he must have been lost at some point in his life—as a child, perhaps—but it was an alien concept to him now.

Every trail he'd ever followed had led him to where he needed to be.

And now the people who had taken him at the end of that journey needed him and he'd be damned if he would let them down.

He drilled deeper into the focus that had so often kept him and others alive. There was an answer and he would find it.

Nasir had realised, without acknowledging it, that he had been alone for some time, but he expected that all roads, in this case, converged. Find one and he would find them all.

His ears caught a sound on what ought to have been the wind, and his dark eyes flicked upwards. He paused, predator-still, trying to catch the shape of it.

'Nasir!'

The Lady Marion? What was she doing out here?

He bolted towards the sound of her voice, as if intending to outrun it, but was pulled up short by another sound, equally familiar.

Horses. Approaching at speed. Half a dozen. No, a dozen.

The Saracen drew his blades and settled himself in the centre of a self-determined circle. They were coming from all sides. He was surrounded.

He shook his head. *I don't think so.*

Something was wrong about the sound. Galloping hooves. Pounding the ground in threatening rhythm. But there were words there too.

'Black sun. Black sun. Black sun.'

From the depths of a wall of mist, the first of the

horses leapt, obscenely high towards him, a Knight Templar in its saddle, sword at the ready.

Nasir ducked and rolled beneath the beast, slashing at the animal's tendons. With luck, it would crush the rider before he could even rally.

But the blade seemed to slip through the flesh without so much as drawing a drop of blood. The horse was no phantom though. He discovered this as its hind leg caught him a stunning crack on landing, sending him barrelling further into the fog.

He rolled again to avoid the knight's sword and leapt to his feet.

Further riders erupted from the mist, encircling him, as the first knight's gloved fist drove him to his knees. He saw a glint of light as the sword was raised again and wondered briefly at its source.

Nasir closed his eyes in silent prayer. To every god that had treated him kindly. To Herne, Lord of the Trees. To Robin, the Hooded Man. To give his life in the service of the latter was comfort enough.

But the killing blow never fell.

Instead he heard a voice. Marion's voice again.

'The black sun has seen you. Feed the black sun.'

Robin Hood fought to stand still.

Every tendon was screaming at him. Run into the mist. Find your friends and kill those who threaten them. Find Marion and take revenge on those who dared to imperil her.

But Herne's voice had lingered, even as his body had faded from view.

'The realm of dreams awaits you. Free your mind and your body from the chains of fear and the final test can begin.'

'I don't understand.'

'I will guide you. But you are already on your way. You will confront the source and the vessel for the darkness. But you must not run. Like a dream, you must surrender to slumber and allow it to find you.'

'So I must just *wait*.'

'Perhaps the most difficult task I will ever ask you to undertake.'

As far as Little John was concerned, it was typical of his companions to get themselves lost this way. Admittedly, Nasir was usually better at this sort of thing. But Will and Robin were always getting themselves into scrapes like this.

It was a damned good thing they had him to pull their hides from the fire.

'Robin!'

Where *was* he?

'Scarlet! Nasir! Damn it!'

John cursed the fog, loud and long.

'John!'

He turned towards the sound. Two voices, in unison. Marion and... Meg. His heart leapt into his throat.

'Meg?'

'John, I'm lost.' Little John's wife, who ought to have been safe and sound in Wickham, sounded terrified. He felt his blood boil further than before. Whatever faceless horror had brought this down upon them was going to pay.

'Meg, sweetheart. Everything is fine. Are you with Marion?'

'John, please!'

Marion's voice rang through the mists. 'Don't worry, John. She was tending me. I woke up alone and she cared for me.'

'Alone? Tuck and Much were with you.'

'There was no one there but Meg.'

John sighed. That was another two heads he'd have to crack together when he found them. Although it would be just like Meg to go wandering in search of them and end up playing nursemaid, bless her heart.

'Stay where you are,' he called back. 'I'll find you.'

Little John steadied himself. There had to be an answer. They sounded close. He just needed to keep moving and—

The sudden screams came from every direction at once.

'I'm coming! Meg, I'm coming!'

Then the sound of horses. And an unmistakeable, sneering bellow urging them after their quarry.

Gisburne. Bloody Gisburne.

John began to run, panicked, towards the sound.

But before he could get more than a few steps, something—something barbed and venomous—wound its way around his ankle and he fell awkwardly towards a ground he could not see. His head caught the edge of… what? Stone? Wood?

He felt blood form a lazy river across his temple. His eyes were demanding to shut. Before he capitulated, however, he was sure he saw Marion standing over him, her bright, red hair a blaze against the white of the mist.

'*The black sun loves you,*' she whispered. '*Feed the black sun.*'

'Lord, give me patience,' muttered Friar Tuck.

He took as deep a breath as he could muster and screamed once more into the fog.

'Much!'

That boy. Such a good heart, but the things he could do to complicate the simplest task... He couldn't be more than a few feet away.

The friar had quickly abandoned his search for the river, realising that there simply wasn't a way to navigate through the mist. But when he'd tried to retrace his steps, he found himself—as his companions had before him—completely surrounded by white, unyielding walls, through which he could move, but never chart.

He wiped his brow with the rough material of his sleeve, surprised to find he was sweating. He hoped that he wasn't succumbing to the same fever that was tormenting Marion.

The thought of his patient, waiting for him, drove him forward.

A flicker of red in the white caught his eye. It couldn't be—

'Little Flower?' he called out. 'What are you doing up? You need your rest.'

'I've rested enough,' she said, with a laugh. 'Too much sleep. And too much to do.'

There was something about the quality of the voice that set his teeth on edge. *Had the fever made her delirious?*

'Not delirious, dear Friar,' said Marion's voice. But not Marion, Tuck knew now. He'd been her confessor long enough; even her sins, such as they were, had a cast of innocence. There was no evil in that young woman, not a drop, and this voice was drenched in it. Besides, Marion couldn't read his thoughts.

His hand flew to the crucifix around his neck.

'Who are you?'

'Don't you know? You've been chasing me your whole life?'

'Chasing you? I don't think so. I have spent my life trying to drive you out.'

'Serving at the abbot's pleasure? Is that what you call driving me out?'

Tuck laughed. 'Lucifer would choose a sin for which I haven't already done my penance. My conscience is clear.'

54

'That is fortunate for you,' the voice said. 'I suspect a guilty man might not survive.'

And then there was no Marion, no Tuck, no Sherwood, no mist. No hope, no glory, no flesh, no spirit. Just an aching, endless blackness, pouring itself into his throat and his eyes and ears, like hot tar. Choking his screams before they'd even formed. The evil he had once adjured to depart, under his skin. Stealing his name.

Words rose in his gullet, finding no path by which to escape. A verse that had haunted him since childhood:

Eloi Eloi lama sabachthani?

My God, my God, why hast thou forsaken me?

'*The black sun shelters the forsaken,*' no God of his replied. '*Feed the black sun.*'

CHAPTER 4

The mists rolled up and away, like a veil being lifted, as Robin stepped forward.

He had been expecting to find himself in a hellscape, filled with the cries of the damned. Or some terrible wasteland, torn by unjust war. But these were the dark fantasies of his waking life and this, as Herne had warned him, was the realm of dreams.

And in his dreams, always, he was in Sherwood. Sometimes alone, marking a moment, before returning to the hustle and bustle of the camp. Sometimes he and Marion were working together— holding back death itself.

Other times, he walked through the greenwood with his father, the Earl—asking forgiveness one night; decrying his inflexibility another. There were even times when he saw a shadow amongst the trees that he recognised as Robin Hood, though he knew him to be a different man. His brother in Herne, his worthy rival in love and legacy.

He drew a calming breath.

Was that it? Was that the fear he was meant to face here—some lingering insecurity that he had not yet measured up to his predecessor? Was that the spark of greed in him? Did he want another man's past for his own?

No.

He set the thought firmly in his mind, like a monument. He was Robin Hood. Herne's son. And those who wore the hood before him were part of him. If this power thought it could tempt him into petty jealousy over the men, over the woman, that had accepted him in the heat of their grief it was too late- that test had come and gone.

His hand flew to Albion as the anger caught fire.

And a laugh, light as a feather, fluttered through the forest.

'I can see why Herne chose you,' said Marion, stepping from behind an ancient oak. For a moment, Robin imagined he had seen a face in the gnarled bark of the tree itself, a mirror image of the Marion he knew—mocking and cruel. 'You're terribly amusing. Such fascinating little thoughts.

So enamoured of the inconsequential. Life and death. Love and grief.' She spat the last few words, as though the taste of them disgusted her.

Robin's rage grew. It was Marion's tongue, her lips, but not her voice. Whatever spoke now was taking the lightness, the kindness and the strength of it and twisted it this way and that, trying to determine at which point it might break.

'Release her,' said Robin.

'And predictable too. I'd say it was disappointing, but, in truth, it's comforting. Your kind have always been so easy to read. Always rushing between the light and the shadow, in search of something you couldn't find in the other.'

Robin drew Albion from its sheath.

'I said, release her.'

Marion's hand made a gentle, almost casual motion, as if brushing away a fly. Albion leapt from Robin's hand and thrust itself deep into a nearby tree in a burst of flame.

'Magic swords? I imagined the children might have outgrown their toys by now. Try again.'

'Who are you?'

'An intelligent question, at last. My name, for your purposes, is Lunis. Queen of the Black Sun. A sun that burns so brightly in your wasted sky. I've been waiting for you, gatekeeper. We have much to discuss.'

'I shall speak of nothing to you until you release Marion.'

'And stubborn. How wonderful.' She stripped her borrowed voice of all pretence of humanity. 'What a feast you will make for the black sun.'

'I fear I am underprepared for such an honour.'

'Enough. Your prattling was an interesting distraction, Hooded Man, but the time of the black sun is upon you. You have come, as the prophecy said you would. So, let us proceed.'

'You speak of prophecy. You say this is foreordained. And you clearly have great power. Yet, I have never heard your name spoken before.'

It was a glancing blow, but found its mark, nonetheless.

Lunis glared at him.

'Is that so—I am forgotten to the world of man?' She clicked the bones in Marion's neck with a series of movements that sickened Robin's eye. 'Unfortunate, but easily undone.'

Greed, said Herne's voice, in Robin's head. *Greed and fear. You must face them both.*

'Why has Herne never spoken of you?' said Robin, playing for time. 'If I am to be gatekeeper, it would be wise for me to know what I'm meant to keep out.'

'Because Herne and all his kind would wipe me from the record, to blot out the deeds they had to undertake in order to bind me.'

'There is always war. There are always battles to fight.'

'In your world, yes. You war because you desire power, because you lust after it. You take it from one another like squabbling babes in the cradle. When the black sun shone above, there was no battle for power. There *was* power. *I* was power. You talk of Herne and his ilk as the Old Gods, when they are nothing but petty usurpers. We were the Gods of Old, before the chaining of the darkness. When men lived in fear but knew it not, for they had never known peace. When they cloaked themselves in blood and darkness at our whim, feeding the very sun that had driven them to each act of madness. You talk of battles? Of glory? There is no glory in your so-called war. It is nothing but a child's impression of ruling.'

'If you were so powerful, then how did you fall?'

'Light came. Vicious, stinging, burning light. You talk of it as though it is a righteous force, yet it has so much blood on its hands. New Gods, whispering in the ears of those who had never known the concept of peace, of right or wrong. Stirring up dissent and rebellion. Bringing with them, most heinous of all, the merciful release of death. Death is an agent of light, Hooded Man. That thing you rail against most violently. It belongs to Herne and his New Gods. And it stalked us. Tore us from our rightful places. But some of us were too powerful to erase completely. Some could only be bound. Left in the bowels of the earth until the time came to test the judgement handed down upon them.'

'And I am to be the judge?'

'You are Herne's son. The gatekeeper between the powers of light and darkness. Across your shoulders lie the scales. When you face that which you fear most, will you choose the pain of the light or the embrace of the darkness? Will the challenge be proven?'

Robin realised that, as Lunis had spoken, he had begun to alter her face in his mind. He could not do what he clearly needed to do if he believed, in any way, that Marion stood before him.

It was not a fact that had escaped the elder God.

'Robin,' she said. 'Help me.'

And this time, it was Marion. Her voice, her… soul. It dragged Robin roughly from his dreams and into the cold, hard reality of the task before him. She seemed weak, as though, wherever her true self were, it was being drained to… feed the black sun.

'I will accept, as Herne's son, my part in your prophecy. But you must release Marion.'

The life in Marion's eyes grew dim again as Lunis retook control.

'Then you still do not understand the test.'

What do you fear most?

Herne's question rattled in his mind and Robin found himself wishing—not for the first time—that Gods both old and new would show less interest in his affairs.

Losing Marion. He feared losing Marion.

There will be a loss, Herne had said.

He would face his greatest fear and there would be a loss.

No.

Prophecy be damned. That he would not do.

Lunis watched him, eyes darting unnaturally back and forth, as though studying a text.

'Prophecy be damned,' she said. 'Such a wonderful turn of phrase. For a man outside all laws.'

She was reading his thoughts.

'If you know what I'm thinking,' said Robin, 'then where's the test?'

Lunis gave a twist of her wrist—which Robin noted seemed thinner, the skin like parchment that had been left to dry too near a flame—and the mists rolled over them once more.

When the fog parted, they were at Marion's side, in the cave where he had left her. But she no longer slept peacefully. She bucked and moaned as Lunis' fever burned within her. Much sat by her side, desperately holding her hand and failing to restrain his tears.

Robin tried to run to her, but the mists just as quickly snatched them back to the forest. He all but beat his chest in frustration. He closed the distance between himself and this pretender god, finger extended in accusation.

'What have you done to her?'

'Done to her? She is my saviour. She fell prey to desire. In her case, her desire was to share my gold, to save lives. But she desired it all the same. She wanted the feeling of goodness that comes from being able to help people as much as the result. And so she carried me out of that desolate tomb and back to the world. I am bound to her. She is my lifeblood.'

'And you're feeding on her.'

'You don't begrudge the infant at its mother's breast. Why do I deserve less consideration?'

An image rose unbidden in Robin's mind. A child that ought to have given him strength but had become yet another loss for he and Marion to face.[1]

'Because—' he said, trying desperately to put all thoughts of the infant Robyn from his mind before they could be leapt on by his adversary.

Lunis cut him off with a mocking laugh.

'Because you love her? Because she's *good*? Son of Herne, are you not listening? Light and darkness are not good and evil. They are sight and blindness. Men do not change in the light. They simply find themselves places to hide. With me. And yet you set yourself up as gatekeepers, as judge, jury and executioner. When I am the honest traveller and you are the thief.'

'What do you want from me?'

'I want you to upset the balance you have unfairly set in place and let men be truthful again.'

'How?'

'Become my champion.'

'And you will set Marion free.'

---

1   See *What Was Lost* by Iain Meadows (on audio, read by Jason Connery), adapted by Elliot Thorpe as a novella.

'On the contrary, she and I will become one. And you will never suffer her loss. You will never see her perish at the end of an arrow, or wither and die in old age. She and I will rule with you at our side.'

'In darkness.'

'In truth.'

'And if I refuse?'

'Then I will continue to feed on her until she is drained beyond recognition. And then I will move on to the next and the next and the next, until the next Hooded Man is selected and makes a wiser choice. Many will suffer. Many will die. Unjustly. Without cause. Is that not the mantle you have taken on? The scourge of the unjust?'

What is your greatest fear?

'If I were to kill you—'

Lunis outstretched her arm and Albion flew to her. She hefted the sword towards Robin. He caught it warily.

'Then she too would die, yes.'

'Those are my choices, are they?' Robin inquired. 'Become your champion and Marion and I will live forever. Kill you and she dies.'

Lunis smiled and any remaining thought of her and Marion as the same vanished. There was nothing of Marion in that smile. No light. No happiness.

I ask you again. What is your greatest fear? What do you desire so much, that the fear of losing it would turn you to darkness?

No light. No happiness.

A life without loss. A life without death or pain.

That was the dowry for his betrayal. Forsake Herne and remove all threat of suffering from the woman he loved.

He was greedy for Marion's happiness. *Yes, my son.* He feared causing her any further pain. As the first Hooded Man had done before him. He feared sacrificing himself in the cause of life, not because he valued his own existence, but because he valued her happiness. A happiness on which he had impinged far too often.

Robin smiled.

Marion lurched upright from the cave floor, her eyes wide and staring. Much stumbled backwards against the stone, his head connecting with a thud.

'Robin! No!' she screamed.

'You've taken a woman's form. Stolen her voice and her appearance. But you don't understand Marion at all.'

Robin held Albion at arm's length, its point towards Lunis' throat.

'I see Herne has done his work well,' she said, genuinely impressed. 'You would sacrifice your lover for his cause.'

'No,' said Robin. 'I could never do that and Herne would never ask me to. He told me that I would face my greatest fear and that there would be a loss. And, as you described, I thought I would suffer a loss. I thought my fears were for myself. You say light and darkness are sight and blindness. I say they are love and…'

'Hate?' hissed Lunis.

'Solitude,' said Robin. 'Think how you punished us. Tearing Marion and I from each other. Because that's what angers you. Not that men and women can turn away from the darkness, but that they lead each other *away* from the darkness. That they can care for others more than they do for themselves. Because you have never cared for anyone and no one has ever cared for you. They locked you away and no one even blinked an eye. No worshippers weeping at their altars. No scribes setting down ballads. Just forgotten.'

'They will return.'

'They don't even remember your name.'

Lunis screamed and the mist descended, only now it coiled and writhed like serpents.

Robin stood his ground.

'Marion is going to fight you.' Robin felt certain he was right as he spoke. 'I don't know if it will be enough, but she knows love and she knows what love can do. And to stop it, she will fight you.'

Lunis' form began to flicker in front of his eyes, the façade of Marion falling away to reveal something that words refused to cling too, a creature that looked like emptiness and smelled of despair.

'She's pulling away, isn't she?' Robin stepped closer, Albion poised to strike. 'Because the other thing you can't comprehend is that she would never choose to live in darkness. Not for eternity, not for a day. Because she is light. She is good. And I will break her heart if it allows her to remain that way.'

Robin twisted Albion away from Lunis and placed the point at his own chest.

'If I must face my greatest fear, then I do so gladly. The fear that she will never forgive me for what I do to save her.'

With one swift thrust, Robin drove the sword into his own chest.

'Robin!'

Marion leapt up, her heart thudding. Much lay slumped in a heap against the wall, unconscious but visibly breathing.

She couldn't keep her thoughts straight. It was as though she'd seen it with her own eyes. As though she'd watched Robin plunge the blade into his chest—and she was powerless to stop him.

She'd taunted him. She'd baited him. And so he'd done it for her.

Her hands flew to her face and, as they did, Marion noticed the dark, charred remains of the gemstone still clinging to her palms.

She rubbed them together roughly, but the grains seemed to embed themselves further into her skin.

Her eyes flew wildly around the cave. No water. Nothing to cleanse the stain of Lunis from her.

And then she saw the fire. And in the fire, a face. A travesty of face, screeching and cursing, but hanging onto life.

What is your greatest fear, daughter of the forest?

To lose him. To lose him again. To lose any more than I already have.

You have never lost him. Not the man he was before. Nor, if you answer honestly, the man he is now.

To abandon him. As I have done before. To disrespect the sacrifices we have made, all of us. To run from the pain.

Face that fear.

Marion thrust her hands into the fire.

EPILOGUE

The Queen of the Black Sun awoke in darkness.

In silence.

There had been a man. A woman. A test of wills.

There had been light.

The memory of that light, the heat and the warmth of it, kept rising in her mind, however hard she tried to push it away.

She was a creature of darkness. She belonged to the darkness. To the black sun.

Why was she weeping for the absence of the light?

This was not her. This was not her destiny.

She was…

Her wail increased in volume.

She had forgotten her name.

In Sherwood Forest, at the crest of a hill, at the end of a storm, seven dreamers awoke.

They stretched their limbs and cricked their backs and found themselves grateful that any morning mist had already lifted.

The sky above them was clear.

Marion's eyes opened last, for she had the most to dread.

Robin's were wide open from the beginning.

They stood and faced each other, their silence louder than the others could bear.

'Was it all a dream?' Much only spoke to break the tension.

'If it were a dream, you dolt,' said Will, 'then why would we all be having it?'

'I didn't say it was a good dream.'

'What does that have to do—?' Will broke off as his eyes turned to Marion and Robin.

'I saw you die.' Marion spoke softly, tears pricking at her eyes as she reached out to Robin. 'I made you die.'

'Hold on,' said Little John. 'What's all this about dying?'

'Do you understand why?' Robin ignored John for the moment, his gaze fixed on Marion.

'I mean it,' John insisted, but Nasir nudged him and held a finger to his lips.

'I understand,' said Marion. 'Do I have to like it?'

'No.'

'Then thank you.' She smiled as they held each other close, both feeling the sense of safety and rightness that being together brought with it.

A droplet of rain fell onto the back of Much's hand. He looked up at the sky, where perfectly ordinary clouds were beginning to gather.

'I think it's going to rain,' he said. 'Should we find shelter?'

'No!' came the reply, in unison. Then a wave of laughter broke through the ranks.

'I was only asking,' Much muttered.

Tuck patted him on the shoulder. 'I think we can stand a little rain.'

You may also enjoy...

Richard Carpenter's

ROBIN OF SHERWOOD

HERE BE DRAGONS

Gary Russell

You may also enjoy...

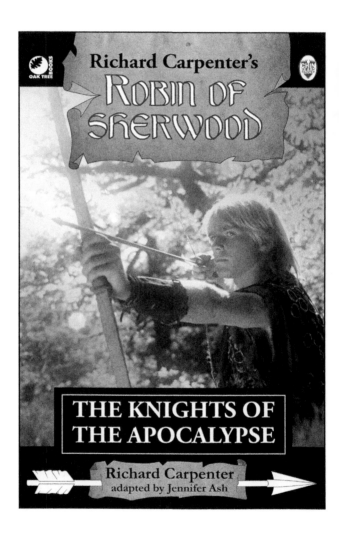

Richard Carpenter's
ROBIN OF
SHERWOOD

THE KNIGHTS OF
THE APOCALYPSE

Richard Carpenter
adapted by Jennifer Ash

You may also enjoy...

Richard Carpenter's

ROBIN OF
SHERWOOD

THE
POWER OF
THREE

Jennifer Ash

You may also enjoy...

Richard Carpenter's
ROBIN OF SHERWOOD

THE
MEETING
PLACE

Jennifer Ash

Printed in Great Britain
by Amazon

52087405R00047